SLIP STREAM

STUNT RIDERS

DAVID AND HELEN ORME
Illustrated by ANDREW WILDMAN

EDGE
FRANKLIN WATTS
LONDON·SYDNEY

First published in 2012 by
Franklin Watts
338 Euston Road
London NW1 3BH

Franklin Watts Australia
Level 17/207 Kent Street
Sydney NSW 2000

A CIP catalogue record for this book is
available from the British Library.

ISBN 978 1 4451 1314 2

Series Editors: Adrian Cole and Jackie Hamley
Series Advisors: Diana Bentley and Dee Reid
Series Designer: Peter Scoulding

1 3 5 7 9 10 8 6 4 2

Printed in China

Franklin Watts is a division of
Hachette Children's Books,
an Hachette UK company.
www.hachette.co.uk

CONTENTS

CHAPTER 1

STUNT BIKE SHOW

Dan wanted to be a stunt motorbike rider.

One day he saw a poster.

Dan couldn't miss this show!

CHAPTER 2
DEATH RISK

The crowd wanted to see Zak and Jed risk death.

The riders roared out, dressed in black.

The stunts were amazing.

Zak rode a motorbike along a wire.

Everyone thought he would fall.

9

The next stunt was the exploding coffin.

Jed got into the coffin.

5! 4! 3! 2! 1!

Then the coffin blew up.

Jed was trapped! He was a mass of flames.

Zak rode into the flames to save Jed!

Everyone screamed.

Then they came roaring out! It was just a stunt!

The crowd cheered.

CHAPTER 3
JUST LIKE YOU

The crowd had gone.

At the end of the field was a caravan.

Dan banged on the door.

He could see Jed in the caravan but

Jed didn't answer.

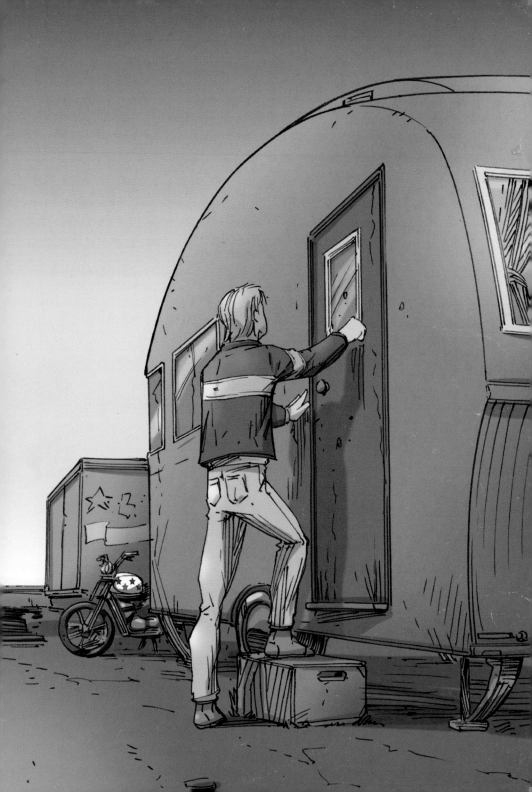

"I want to be a stunt rider like you…" said Dan.

Then Dan heard a voice behind him. It was Zak.

"Let's see what you can do," he said.

CHAPTER 4
STUNT RIDER

"Ride up that ramp," said Zak.

Dan climbed on a bike. He roared up the ramp.

"I must hold it steady and keep the wheel straight,"

he thought.

Dan got to the top of the ramp.

"Not bad," said Zak. "Come back tomorrow."

CHAPTER 5

DEAD FAMOUS

The next day Dan banged on the caravan door.

There was no answer. Dan went in.

He saw an old newspaper on the table.

"But Zak and Jed aren't dead," said Dan.

"Oh yes we are," said Zak.

Dan turned round.

Zak and Jed were standing by the door.

"You can't do stunts like ours if you are alive," said Jed.

"Now you can be a stunt rider like us," said Zak.

"You can go in the exploding coffin."

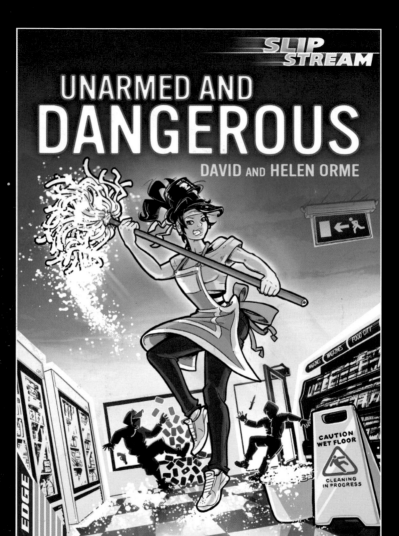

Nita wants to go out, but her dad says she has
to help in the shop. So Nita decides to have some fun!

Nita's fun leads to a big mess and her dad
is not happy. Then two robbers rush into
the shop. Can Nita stop them?

EDGE **FRANKLIN** **WATTS** **W**

LONDON·SYDNEY

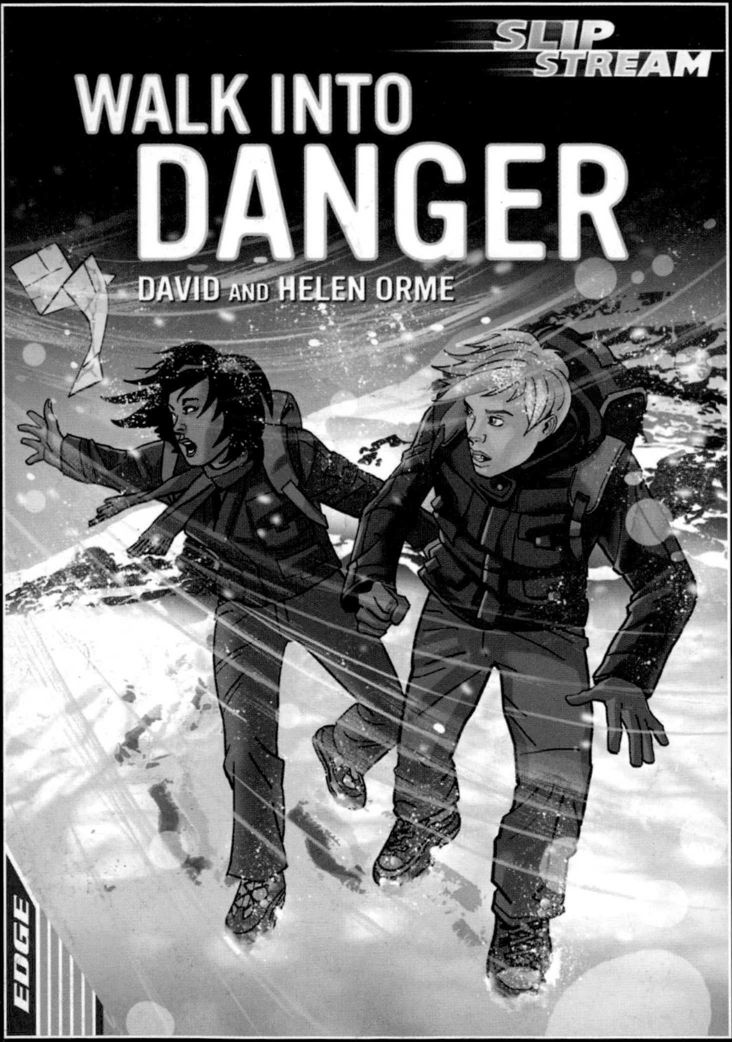
SLIP STREAM
WALK INTO
DANGER
DAVID AND HELEN ORME
EDGE

Simon and Lia are on a hike, but they get lost.
It starts to snow and they can't see the path.

They hear a voice calling. A man
has broken his leg. Simon and Lia must
find a way to get help, before it's too late...

LONDON·SYDNEY

About

SLIP STREAM

Slipstream is a series of expertly levelled books designed for pupils who are struggling with reading. Its unique three-strand approach through fiction, graphic fiction and non-fiction gives pupils a rich reading experience that will accelerate their progress and close the reading gap.

At the heart of every Slipstream fiction book is a great story. Easily accessible words and phrases ensure that pupils both decode and comprehend, and the high interest stories really engage older struggling readers.

Whether you're using Slipstream Level 1 for Guided Reading or as an independent read, here are some suggestions:

1. Make each reading session successful. Talk about the text before the pupil starts reading. Introduce any unfamiliar vocabulary.

2. Encourage the pupil to talk about the book using a range of open questions. For example, what would be their dream job?

3. Discuss the differences between reading fiction, graphic fiction and non-fiction. What do they prefer?

Slipstream Level 1 photocopiable **WORKBOOK** ISBN: 978 1 4451 1609 9 available – download free sample worksheets from: www.franklinwatts.co.uk

For guidance, SLIPSTREAM Level 1 – Stunt Riders has been approximately measured to:

National Curriculum Level: 2c
Reading Age: 7.0–7.6
Book Band: Turquoise

ATOS: 1.9*
Guided Reading Level: H
Lexile® Measure (confirmed): 290L

*Please check actual Accelerated Reader™ book level and quiz availability at www.arbookfind.co.uk